I0538284

Reflections

By Yaasha Moriah

Copyright @ 2015 Yaasha Moriah
Published: 1 November 2015

ISBN 978-0-98-920012-7

Print Edition
Printed by CreateSpace

Cover design by Yaasha Moriah

Cover photos by:
"Lighthouse" © Bonnybbx | Pixabay.com
"Archangel Michael" © Deleuran | Pixabay.com
"Galaxy" © Chrystal-e | Pixabay.com
"Mirror Frame" © Sannys_Stocks | Deviantart.com

Find out more about the author and upcoming books online at **www.YaashaMoriah.com** or @YaashaMoriah.

for the Scribe,
who gave me a pen and taught me to reflect his
words rightly

for my father,
who would not let me reflect less than my potential

Then He called out in my hearing with a loud voice, saying, "Let those who have charge over the city draw near, each *with* a deadly weapon in his hand." **2** And suddenly six men came from the direction of the upper gate, which faces north, each with his battle-ax in his hand. **One man among them *was* clothed with linen and had a writer's inkhorn at his side.** They went in and stood beside the bronze altar.

3 Now the glory of the God of Israel had gone up from the cherub, where it had been, to the threshold of the temple.[a] **And He called to the man clothed with linen, who *had* the writer's inkhorn at his side; 4 and the Lord said to him, "Go through the midst of the city, through the midst of Jerusalem, and put a mark on the foreheads of the men who sigh and cry over all the abominations that are done within it."**

5 To the others He said in my hearing, "Go after him through the city and kill; do not let your eye spare, nor have any pity. **6** Utterly slay old *and* young men, maidens and little children and women; but **do not come near anyone on whom *is* the mark**; and begin at My sanctuary." So they began with the elders who *were* before the temple. **7** Then He said to them, "Defile the temple, and fill the courts with the slain. Go out!" And they went out and killed in the city.

8 So it was, that while they were killing them, I was left *alone;* and I fell on my face and cried out, and said, "Ah, Lord God! Will You destroy all the remnant of Israel in pouring out Your fury on Jerusalem?"

9 Then He said to me, "The iniquity of the house of Israel and Judah *is* exceedingly great, and the land is full of bloodshed, and the city full of perversity; for they say, 'The Lord has forsaken the land, and the Lord does not see!' **10** And as for Me also, My eye will neither spare, nor will I have pity, *but* I will recompense their deeds on their own head."

11 Just then, the man clothed with linen, who *had* the inkhorn at his side, reported back and said, "I have done as You commanded me."

Table of Contents

I

A Story in Runes

"Don't look at the water!" Richard screamed, snatching Margaret away from the edge of the boardwalk. Her skin crawled with cold sweat. He pushed her forward. Her feet slipped on the slime that dribbled at the edges of the warping wooden planks of the boardwalk, which receded into the twilight mist like a road that led to the edge of the world.

"Are we almost there?" Elizabeth gasped, hugging herself, almost incoherent. "Please tell me we're almost there."

"How should I know?" Richard snapped. "I've never been here before."

"Just follow the boardwalk," Robert said, his tone unraised but constricted.

"We'll never make it," Elizabeth began to sob, a high-pitched keening sound. "He's going to find us…"

"Shut up!" Richard turned on her savagely. "Just shut up! And why wear yellow? Of all things, why yellow?"

Elizabeth clutched her head through the daffodil-colored hoodie. Her shoulder-length black hair clung to her face where the tears had run.

"He's not hunting by sight," Robert reminded abruptly. "The Scribe said…"

"To Hades with the Scribe!" Richard spun again. "The sooner we reach the Sender, the better."

"What if he can't do anything?" Margaret's lips were pale as she shuddered violently. "You know it's only a matter of time."

"Look, if you want to second-guess the plan, go ahead!" Richard spat. "Wait here until he finds you and do what he did to Tina. Or worse. Probably worse."

"What's that?" Robert leaped back from the edge of the boardwalk. Elizabeth and Richard screamed. The swamp and the mist swallowed their cries.

Richard recovered first and cursed. "Robert, you idiot! It was just a frog."

Robert closed his eyes and swallowed hard.

"How do you know it was a frog?" Margaret challenged. "You didn't look in the water, did you? Did you?"

"Don't look at the water," Elizabeth murmured, her hands on either side of her face like blinders. "Don't look at the water. Don't look at the water."

Richard shoved past them, red-faced. "Curse the Sender! Why build a hut in the middle of a stinking swamp?"

"Because," said a voice. "I prefer to be left alone."

* * * * *

"That's where the runes end," RC murmured. "There's nothing more to translate."

"Are you sure that's what it said?" his mother, Ellie, asked, her high cheekbones outlined harshly by the light of the rechargeable lamp, which had been placed in a slight recession in the wall. "That seems more like part of a story. It's not consistent with ancient Fulmian thought patterns at all. Too much emotion. Too much fear."

"I translated; this is what it said." RC tapped his electronic pad with the stylus, irritated and vaguely disturbed.

"Greta? Your thoughts?" Ellie asked. "You're the cultural expert, after all. I'm just an archaeologist."

"It's… I don't know." Greta's rich alto voice came slowly, as she squinted at the runes on the stone door. "I agree. It doesn't seem Fulmian. But… It's strange. I feel that I've heard that story before, a long time ago. Maybe it's part of a Fulmian legend I studied at the university."

Ellie shrugged. "We'll ask Bob when he gets back."

"Ask me what?" Bob ducked as he descended the steps of gray stone into the narrow passageway. "Did you finish the translation, RC?"

"I did," RC said, a little stiffly.

"Difficult?"

"Actually, ridiculously easy."

"Hmm, that's odd. I thought you'd at least get hung up on the compound words. I spotted quite a few of them. Syllabic languages can be tricky." Bob's puff of white hair and his well-groomed mustache caught the light of the lamp and threw it back at the darkness, ringing his face with a halo of light.

"Could you translate the first few lines, sir?" RC asked.

"A little self-conscious for a teenage genius, don't you think?" Bob smiled, unscrewing the top of his thermos and pouring steaming coffee into the cap. "You should go first. Impress me."

"Just the first few lines, please." RC tapped nervously with his stylus again.

Bob sipped, then shrugged. He pulled oval glasses out of his breast pocket and perched them on his nose. "Eh, let's humor the boy. Let's see. It

4

starts off with ta-kum-ta go-ha—'I the one and only warrior'—be-ya-tu-sa-yee. Now, depending on how you combine the syllables, you could get a number of different translations. Beya Tusayee would be Justice-bringer or Avenger. Be Yatu Sayee would be Gold of Death. Or you could have Beyatu Sa Yee: Mirror of Evil. What did you come up with, RC?"

RC reddened and lowered his e-pad.

"I'd like a little more time to translate, sir."

Bob smiled a little and patted RC's shoulder. "Go slowly, boy. Languages take time to learn well."

Bob and Greta turned their attention to the door with the runes, and RC retreated to the steps. Ellie joined him.

"Honey, everyone makes mistakes…"

"It doesn't make sense!" RC exploded. "I saw it. I went over and over it. That's what the runes said. You think I'd make that up? Who wants to look stupid?"

"RC, no one is calling you stupid."

"I *saw* it. But then Bob… And when he explained it… It's like the runes changed."

"Maybe we need better lighting."

"If Bob can read it, I can read it!" RC rose abruptly and charged up the steps. Bob and Greta glanced at Ellie in surprise, their conversation clipped in mid-sentence. Ellie raised her hands in exasperation.

"Let him be," Bob said gently. "Growing up takes time too."

II

The Beginning of Dreams

"Maggie had another bad dream last night," Aunt Betty murmured over the tinkle of silver spoons on ceramic bowls. Dick's spoon dipped again into the steaming peach pudding and rose to his mouth.

"They're getting more frequent," Aunt Betty pointed out.

Dick swallowed. "So send for a doctor. Find out what's wrong."

"People aren't like things, Dick. You can't just fix them. They're complicated."

Dick dabbed his mouth with a spotless white napkin, the lines around his mouth half-hidden by his full mustache. He met her eyes.

"What do you want me to do? If a doctor can't fix her, I can't."

"Maybe it's something…subconscious. The dreams terrify her. Maybe it's because of your long trips away. Maybe she needs you home."

"She's got her brother."

"Ribs is only seven. Two years younger than her. But you're her *father*."

Dick rose and two attending servants appeared, one who lifted a black coat ceremoniously and a second who proffered a high-topped hat. Dick turned, thrust both arms into the satin-lined sleeves of the coat, and shrugged the coat over his shoulders. He lifted the hat from the servant's hands and placed it firmly over his curly dark hair.

"Aunt Betty, little girls have to grow up sometime."

When he was gone, Aunt Betty hobbled over the multi-colored mosaic floor to the wide, curving staircase that glittered like gold and ivory. Evidence of the master's trade lined the walls and floor—a stone half-nude cherub playing a panpipe, a framed depiction of some mythological battle between a man and a monster, an exquisitely curved vase of lapis lazuli, and many more exceptional specimens of art through the ages.

"It is not a home for children," she muttered under her breath as she mounted the stairs, laboriously. She passed her own portrait on the stairwell, a pose from her younger days when her hair was black and her back straight.

She found the children huddled in a window-seat overlooking the frozen pond in the center of the sleeping garden.

"Maggie's been crying," Ribs announced. "I gave her a handkerchief, but she won't stop."

"Go away," Maggie snapped, her voice muffled. Only her honey-brown curls were visible behind the moist cloth handkerchief. "Where's Papa?"

"He's meeting a man on Courthouse Street. Apparently the party has a *very important* piece of art to sell." Aunt Betty's emphasis laced the words with acid.

Maggie's face, swollen and flushed, emerged from behind the handkerchief.

"I wish he would come home. He's not safe."

"Now, Maggie, why would you say that?" Aunt Betty groaned a little as she lowered herself to the cushioned window-seat and gathered Maggie in her arms. Ribs, not to be ignored, quickly occupied the space on the other side of his great-aunt.

"We're all unsafe," Maggie hiccupped. "He's coming after us."

"Who is coming after us? Darling, is this from your dream?"

Maggie nodded.

"Honey, you should know it's just a dream. No one wants to hurt you in real life."

"But it's true," Maggie insisted. "We're going to die."

A chill seemed to descend upon the room, as though a draft from the wintry garden had entered through the window. Aunt Betty hugged her great-niece tighter.

"Why should we die?"

"Because," said Maggie, her tears reflecting Aunt Betty's pale face. "We did something awful. We did it and we have to pay."

III

At the Foot of the Hanging Tree

He waited for them at the foot of the Hanging Tree, an ancient gnarled oak that dominated the treeline, draped with the remnants of frayed ropes that swung like dreadlocks in the late spring breeze. The stubble of a beard outlined his strong jaw, his cornsilk eyebrows almost invisible over eyes the color of deep ice. He wore oval spectacles; an odd thing, for a woodsman to possess weak eyes. Were it not for his pale features, his patched clothing would have melted him into the thick greens and opaque browns of the Old Forest.

He scanned them as they approached.

"Peggy," said the woman, a little breathlessly, middle age etching the corners of her expressive green eyes. "You must be our guide."

"Bert," said the man bluntly, glancing past her at the others. "Half now."

"What? Oh." Peggy's chin lifted and her gaze upon him sharpened. "Excuse me, please."

Bert ignored her as she sought the modesty of some undergrowth. Like all wise traveling women, she did not carry her money where it could be seen.

The next arrival, a girl no older than twelve, struggled to the top of the hill, her cheeks flushed with exertion.

"Hello," she mumbled, her eyes downcast, her black hair straggling from underneath her shawl.

"Name?"

"Liz."

"Half now."

Meekly, she counted out the sum from a stocking she had tied to her belt. Her toes peeked from her ragged shoes and she shivered a little, though it was a warm enough day.

Bert took the offered coins, then flicked one back at her. She caught it reflexively, as though accustomed to dodging missiles.

"Too much," Bert said. He turned as Peggy emerged from the forest and paid her own due, the tilt of her head a little less angular, her eyes gentler.

She had seen the transaction.

The last traveler arrived in a fit of coughing.

"Just the ol' lungs starting up again," the newcomer attempted a wobbly grin. "It's a grand day for a walk."

Bert did not even have to ask; the coins cascaded into his outstretched hand with a harsh clink.

"You take silver, I hope?" the newcomer asked, squinting up at the guide from a breathless half-crouch.

"I prefer gold, but silver will do."

"Good. Can't stand gold. It's so heavy. Like a coffin."

Peggy half-grinned, perplexed, then shrugged as Bert motioned to them, turned, and melted into the shadows of the forest.

"I didn't catch your name," Peggy said, dropping back to accompany the old man. "I'm Peggy."

"Ricky."

"Where are you headed?"

"The northern coast."

"That is a far way through the forest on foot. Surely it would have been easier to go by ship around the point."

"I prefer to go by foot. Water is evil. Things can look back at you in the water. Things you don't want to see you."

"I'm not sure I understand."

"You know it and I know it. So long as we stay away from them, we are safe. We can live forever."

He laughed a short, barking laugh. "I haven't looked in a mirror for my whole life. I don't even look in other people's eyes."

Peggy frowned, the polite smile slipping from her face. "I'm afraid you've lost me. Stay away from what?"

"Don't you know?" Ricky halted suddenly, as if in surprise. Then he leaned in close, and his voice dropped to a chilling whisper. "From the reflections."

IV

Warrior of Worlds

Tomb of Ancient Fulmian War-Leader Found, blazed the headline of the online journal, followed by the glowing press release announcing the work done by Bob and his team. In the warmth of their shared RV near the tomb site, Ellie, RC, and Greta gathered around Bob's tablet to read the account of their exploits in the mountains once occupied by the ancient Fulmian tribe. A color photograph of the runes on the door accompanied the article, with a summary of the translation.

"Isn't it a little early?" Ellie worried. "We're not even sure on the dating, and we haven't found any records of this warrior in any other Fulmian source."

"We're working on that," Greta murmured, typing rapidly on her laptop as she rested in the corner.

"You've been working on that for weeks," RC grumbled. Greta frowned at her screen and did not answer.

"Quite the colorful account," Bob raised his white eyebrows. "I didn't know I had a degree from Jacob Ericson University."

"I'm not comfortable with the publicity," Ellie muttered.

"When the press smells a story, the press print the story," Bob shrugged. "Premature, perhaps, but it keeps public interest, which keeps the funds flowing."

"We should open the tomb soon," RC suggested. "I'm dying to see what's inside."

"In good time," Bob agreed. "First, we must…"

A sharp cry from Greta stifled all conversation.

"What is it?" RC leaped toward her.

"It's the… What in the…?" Greta stopped. "I apologize. I didn't expect…"

Her voice faded and she seemed to collect herself. She gestured toward her screen.

"I've been researching other records that might shed some light on our Fulmian warrior, using the names Bob identified as possibilities: Avenger, Justice-bringer, Gold of Death, and Mirror of Evil. I've researched in every Fulmian document in the database. I've tried every variation I can think of. I've even broadened my search to include other area tribes, since the Fulmians might have given a courageous enemy warrior a Fulmian burial out of respect. But I found no results."

"Until?" Bob prompted.

"Until I threw out the idea that it was Fulmian at all. I've spent the last 12 hours scanning the entire interworld archive for any keywords associated with our warrior's titles. I got thousands of results. Thousands."

"Hmm, looks like you need to narrow your search," Bob murmured.

"You don't understand. The results don't relate to thousands of possibilities through which we'll have to sift to find the right one. *They all point to the same entity*. I'd say that every major ancient culture on every major world has a record somewhere of our warrior."

"That's impossible!" RC's teenage voice cracked, but he ignored it. "That's saying he's been on hundreds of worlds and done enough notable things on each one to earn recognition in thousands of ancient records. That alone would take dozens, if not hundreds, of lifetimes! It's impossible!"

"We're assuming a single individual," Bob said. "Let's suppose that the identification given on this tomb is not a name, but a title. Perhaps a kind of dynasty, or even a tribe. The Avenger may have been some kind of ancient inter-world policeman, who passed on his title to his successor upon his death. I've never heard of such a thing, but it's always possible."

"The title says, 'I, the one and only warrior,'" RC reminded dubiously.

"A statement of preeminence, of superiority," Bob guessed.

"If there are so many records already," RC asked, "Why hasn't someone cataloged this guy by now? Why is everyone silent?"

"No one believed the ancients capable of inter-world travel, thus I doubt anyone has ever cross-referenced all the records of 'the Avenger.'" Bob's upraised hand prevented RC's next protest. "It will take time to unravel all of the potential implications. Still, it raises many fascinating questions. Greta, I most warmly congratulate... Greta?"

Greta wiped her eyes hastily with her sleeve and slapped her laptop shut.

"What's wrong, honey?" Ellie slid an arm around the other woman's shoulders. Greta rose, thrusting Ellie's arm away, and stepped out of the RV into the palpable dark of the night mountains.

V

Hands of Blood

"She'll grow out of it," the doctor assured Aunt Betty as he gathered his hat and coat in the front lobby. "Many children have these sort of dreams. They are called 'night terrors.' It's nothing to worry about."

"But her insistence that they're real?" Aunt Betty persisted.

The doctor patted her kindly.

"Really, madam, it is nothing. But please, if the problem persists, send for me again. I may be able to prescribe a mild sleeping agent to help her rest without disturbing dreams."

"Thank you," Aunt Betty said, a little doubtfully. The servant showed the doctor out, and the heavy thud of the great oak door behind the visitor seemed like the clang of a dungeon gate.

"What's wrong with me?" Aunt Betty shivered. "The door must have blown in a nasty chill when he went out. Gregoire!"

"Yes, madam?"

"Please bring me another wrap from my room."

"Yes, madam."

As Gregoire mounted the stairs briskly, he halted, his eyes locked upon one of the framed pieces mounted along the stairwell.

"Madam, I apologize for the question, but has your portrait always looked this way? I do not recall this…er…" He glanced inquisitively again at the painting, finishing weakly, "…this…*coloring*."

"What are you talking about?" Aunt Betty's cane tapped as she struggled up the first few steps. "Where?"

Dumbly, Gregoire indicated her youthful portrait. All was the same as ever—the white lace cap, the proper collar, the serene expression, even down to the folded hands. Those hands… Aunt Betty peered closer.

"Good gracious!" she gasped. "It looks like blood! All over my hands! It's even soiled my gown!"

"I am most perturbed, madam," Gregoire flushed. "I hesitate to mention it, but perhaps…"

"Perhaps what, Gregoire? Oh, it's ghastly!"

"Young Robbie fancies himself a painter, madam. I have, on occasion, noticed his artistic efforts on a number of household objects—all, fortunately, redeemable heretofore."

"Yes, it must be Ribs," Aunt Betty murmured. "I shall speak to him directly."

"Very good, madam." Gregoire offered his arm to her, and glanced back at the offending portrait, muttering under his breath, "Oddly realistic. Not like random splashes of red. But what possessed the boy?"

While Gregoire sought the wrap, Aunt Betty tapped on Ribs' bedroom door. "Ribs? It's Aunt Betty."

The bathroom door creaked behind her and she turned to see the little boy in question.

"There you are, Ribs! I want to talk… Child, what is the matter?"

His hand on the glass doorknob trembled, and his eyes stared starkly from a face nearly as pale as the frost on the windowpanes. His voice sounded thin, as if from a body only half-present.

"He said you had blood on your hands. He said I do too."

"What are you talking about?"

"He said you would see the evidence, everywhere. He said we would all see it. But he didn't really speak. I just knew what he was thinking."

"Ribs, stop this nonsense at once!" Aunt Betty clutched her cane until her knuckles blanched. "Now tell me, in plain words, what you are talking about."

REFLECTIONS

"The man in the bathroom mirror. He's come to kill us."

VI

Seeking a Sender

"He's not dangerous," Bert said around a mouthful. "He's too old to be dangerous."

"I didn't say 'dangerous,'" Peggy clarified. "But he makes me uncomfortable."

"So he's a little foggy."

"He's paranoid. It's creepy."

"Give him a few days. By the time we reach the Pools, he'll have breath only for the journey."

Peggy sighed. "You're right. I'm probably blowing this out of proportion."

Bert took another mouthful of squirrel and tuber stew, spit out a squirrel rib, and tossed it into the fire, where it snapped like a dry twig.

At that moment, Ricky called from the other side of the fire, "No secret conversations, please! If we're going to travel through the forest together, we should all be good friends!"

Everyone stared at him with eyes dull with fatigue.

"Well, he recovers his breath quickly enough," Peggy muttered to Bert, who grunted in reply.

"I propose introductions!" Ricky announced. "Where are we from and where are we going? Bert, as our valuable host, you first!"

"No," said Bert, picking his teeth with a sliver of wood.

"I'll go first," said the young girl, Liz, unexpectedly. Then she flinched, as though expecting to be struck, but Peggy encouraged her.

"Yes, dear, please tell us about yourself!"

"I was born in a small village," Liz said. "My father, a cheesemaker, died when our donkey kicked him in the head. My mother took me to the city, where she found work in the kitchens. When she died of a fever, I continued to work as a scullery maid."

"It's a hard job," Peggy said quietly.

"It was a job," Liz replied. "It was better than sleeping on the street."

"Of course, of course," Ricky nodded. "And I see you saved up enough to take a trip."

"Yes, barely. I'm going to the coast to see the Sender there."

The news electrified the company, with the exception of Bert, who kept his feelings to himself.

"A Sender! What do you want with a Sender?" Ricky gasped.

"Senders are very expensive," Peggy observed. "And you would need another one to get home."

24

"But that's just it," said Liz. "I don't know if this world *is* my home."

"What do you mean? You just said your parents…" Peggy's words halted in her throat when Bert touched her shoulder, as though to restrain her. His gaze was fixed upon the girl.

Liz seemed to search for words. "I never felt that my life is…thick enough. It feels stretched out or...or sliced. Like my life is only one part of a greater existence. I feel as though it isn't even my own. Things that should have deep importance, like my parents, never seemed like a part of me or my life."

"But how could a Sender help with this?" Ricky asked.

Liz hesitated, then continued: "I overheard a stranger once speaking to my master. The stranger said that the paleness of a life indicates that we belong in another world, that our real existence is imprinted in another place. I decided then that I would get enough money to see a Sender, someone who knows the many worlds in the universe. Maybe the Sender could help me to find the world where I really belong. Maybe he could send me there."

"Who was this stranger?" Bert probed.

"I don't know his name," Liz replied. "But he wore a white robe and carried an inkhorn by his side. I think he was a scrivener."

The color drained from Ricky's face and the shadows in Bert's jaw deepened.

"The Scribe," Ricky said hoarsely. "Which means *he's here already*."

VII

In the Hand of God

Ellie found Greta on the staircase that descended into the wool-like darkness of the "Avenger's tomb," as they now called it. A streak of salt betrayed the trail of a tear past the deep lines of Greta's mouth.

"I feel like a fool," Greta said as Ellie sank onto the step beside her.

"But you aren't one," Ellie replied. "I saw the picture on the laptop before you closed it. Something about that island of rock brought up bad memories for you. I won't pry, but I want you to know that I'm here to listen if you want to talk about it."

"I haven't talked about it for ages. I haven't even *thought* of it for twenty-five years."

"Maybe that means it's time to think about it."

"Some things are so clear. Other things…I can't even remember."

"That's okay. Take your time."

Greta hugged one knee to her chest and closed her eyes, tilting her head back as though to relieve a neck-ache.

*   *   *   *   *

The island is called The Hand of God, in the world known as Esoptron. Formed of rough volcanic black rock, the island is shaped like a great bowl, with five spires that resemble fingers and a thumb, from which its name is derived. An ancient verse accompanies the island, which, roughly translated, proceeds like this:

> *Mirror, mirror, of the worlds,*
> *Speak the verdict: Who is fair?*
> *Witness, memories of time,*
> *What is now and what was then.*
> *Gold will tell what fate is mine:*
> *Stroke of sword, or stroke of pen.*
> *Mirror, mirror, of the worlds,*
> *Who will thy reflection spare?*

My friend Tina and I were both studying social archaeology at Aletheia University on the coast of Esoptron's largest continent. The university was only a few hours away from the archipelago nearest to the Hand of God. Both of us were greatly intrigued by the stories we heard of the island through the native peoples who passed through the college city to and from the archipelago. They seemed to hold it in great reverence and it was said that a great warrior guarded the island.

Despite the island's influence in the culture, it was not covered in any of our course materials. Tina and I received very unsatisfactory answers to our inquiries within the archaeology department. What we eventually grasped was that it had never been explored or studied because of the fears of the native peoples.

We knew that archaeology simply isn't stopped by local fears. A search of the records related to the island revealed that teams had indeed visited the island—and never returned. We disbelieved the stories about a curse and figured that some fanatical group of natives killed the scientists. The few people who claimed to have been to the island seemed to experience marked personality changes, and disappeared soon after their visit to the island.

The island grew on our minds until Tina and I could no longer ignore it. We shared our plan with some of our trusted friends, hired a boat, and headed out to the island. It was foolish—I know that now—but at the time, it seemed like the great archaeological adventure that I had always wished for. We timed our arrival for the deepest part of a moonless night, and anchored on the side of the island opposite the majority of the archipelago.

There, with a few muted lights, we prepared for our entry into the island.

Aerial photographs had shown that the island was completely rock, with very little vegetation, and with only a shallow hollow in the "palm" of the "hand." However, geophysicists from previous teams had determined that the inside of the island was hollow, and that a single underwater passage led to what appeared to be an above-water chamber, about twenty feet high. Additionally, the natives believed in the existence of a chamber filled with cursed gold.

We had come well-prepared. Tina and I had done some diving in the past, and Tina was also the captain on the women's college swim team, so we slipped into our diving suits, with head cameras, and dove down.

The clarity of the water allowed us to see down sixty, seventy, maybe even eighty feet to the bottom, which rippled with pink sand. The island rose from the sea floor like a sheer cliff-face, vertical and uniform. As we passed into the shade of the island, scanning the rock-face for the underwater passage, I instantly felt a stab of cold, despite the insulation in my suit. I am not an imaginative sort, but it felt as though the cold were a sentient thing, a malevolent force.

As we approached the mouth of the passageway, the beams of our headlamps were thrown back into our eyes in a gleam of gold. Swimming closer, we observed that a ten-foot-tall statue of a golden angel guarded the opening. He was dressed as though for war, and his hair fell to his shoulders. His left hand grasped his scabbard, and his right hand curled around the hilt of his sword, as though he were about to draw the sword from its sheath. His wings were folded behind him, but seemed to be in the act of opening, as though in warning.

The eyes puzzled me. They were completely blank. Many sculptors, even ancient ones, set stones in their statues for eyes, or carve irises and pupils. The astounding level of detail in the rest of the statue sharply contrasted with the complete inattention to his eyes. Oddly enough, I had the distinct feeling that they drew me in toward him. You see, detailed eyes express the person; they project personality, even in statues. The flow is *outward*. These eyes, by their very blankness, seemed to reverse the flow, to pull *inward*.

I wondered how the ancient peoples could have possibly created such a detailed statue. With what we knew of their skills, it was nearly impossible that this statue was their own creation. Furthermore, it was unthinkable that thieves had not stolen the statue long ago. Surely, unscrupulous treasure-hunters would have at least tried, or at least hacked off an arm, if the statue proved too heavy to lift with their equipment. But the angel looked utterly untouched, even by the scouring of the waves and sand.

Tina and I swam around the angel several times, to be sure that our cameras fully documented its intricacies. We were thorough, but neither of us wished to linger. Then we entered the passageway.

At first, all was dark, save for our twin shafts of light, striking through the blackness. The passageway narrowed and I swam behind Tina. Our headlamps alighted upon gold again, and there was another statue, his wings spread a little further, his sword sliding from its sheath. I began to feel as if I had very little air left in my tank, but I struggled onward.

After a few minutes, we came upon a third angel. This time, the sword was half-unsheathed, gleaming as though it cast a light of its own. The walls of the passageway lit with shifting threads of gold as our light rippled liquidly from the statue. A sense of claustrophobia, of being watched, of unbearable cold, of intense pressure stacked around me like bricks. I swallowed the hysteria.

Suddenly, our light disappeared. Both of our headlamps, simultaneously, simply switched off. I panicked. Then I realized that I could still see, just a little bit. I glanced up, through the water, and observed that the water ended in a gentle pool. Dark steps led to a sort of dais, or altar. Upon this dais stood another golden angel, with his sword drawn. Behind him, between two pillars of twisted gold, I saw *something*. It was like a vertical surface of water, shimmering and bending. The light source seemed to emanate from it, casting colors upon the walls of the circular chamber.

Tina had reached the edge of the water, and was preparing to lift herself out and approach the angel. That's when I realized that she wore nothing. Nothing at all. No suit. No oxygen tank. No headlamp. *Nothing.*

Suddenly frightened, I kicked toward the surface, to call out to her to come back. As I stroked upward, I caught sight of my own arm—bare and white. I was naked also. Frantically, I searched the sandy bottom of the pool for my gear, but it was gone.

I do not know exactly what happened after that. I remember blindly kicking and struggling through the water, groping through the passageway. To this day, I do not know how I survived without my oxygen tank.

A glow like gold accompanied me, for the angels stood at intervals and seemed to reflect, or generate, a heavy yellow light. But this time their poses were different. One angel's fingers seemed to reach out to grasp me. I pushed past it, and, just a few yards later, nearly swam into another angel, which held up his hand as though to stop me. I glanced back, suddenly irrationally afraid that the grasping angel was coming from behind—but it had disappeared. I dodged past the other angel, and looked back, but it, too, was gone.

The thought arrived so strongly, so palpable, that I could not ignore it. I knew in that instant— *knew*—that there was only one angel. Not many. Just *one*.

The next thing I knew, human hands grasped my wrists, my lungs burned with air, and I slipped into the bottom of a boat. Someone threw a blanket over my shivering body. I heard voices around me, but I could not discern them. I simply stared at the clear cloudless sky, and wondered when it had become day.

Richard was badly frightened. I had been away for almost twelve hours—although it seemed like no more than an hour or two—and my camera feed had discontinued after the first hour, apparently just after we had encountered the angel at the door and had entered the passageway.

Richard's fear made him angry and he belabored me with questions, which I hardly knew how to answer. Finally, Robert pulled him away, advised him to compose himself, and spoke calmly to me.

After I told my story, Robert explained that they, also, had seen the angel. It first appeared on one of the "fingers" of the island, as though observing them from above. Then it was gone, reappearing an hour later at the bottom of the ocean, eighty feet down in the crystal water, its sword stretched toward the boat. When I told them about my experience with the angel, Richard insisted that we must leave at once. I agreed.

Robert strongly opposed us. We had to wait for Tina. A sharp disagreement, spoken only in spooked whispers, arose between us. Elizabeth, rarely one to take sides, agreed first with one, then another. Richard's temper and my fear were no match for Robert's insistence. In the end, we waited.

*   *   *   *   *

After a brief silence, Ellie murmured, "What happened next?"

Greta inhaled deeply through her nose. "Everything after that is a blank. All I recall is that something very terrible happened."

"So when you saw the picture of the island…"

A shudder passed down Greta's spine like a centipede. Ellie waited for a moment, then asked, "Will you come inside? I'll make you a hot cup of coffee."

Greta closed her eyes and breathed deeply.

"I'll come."

Ellie helped Greta to her feet and kept a light grip on her friend's elbow until they reached the RV.

VIII

The Scribe

Aunt Betty was disturbed from her afternoon cogitations in the parlor chair by the sharp rap of the brass doorknocker.

"Gregoire! The door!"

No Gregoire appeared and, after repeated attempts to recall him to his duty, Aunt Betty roused herself and shuffled painfully to the lobby, cane tapping. Panting, she tugged open the heavy oaken door.

"Yes?"

The man who stood upon her doorstep had shocking taste. Who, especially in winter, would wear a *white* suit? Even so, the master would have found the visitor an artistic curiosity. His full, dark curls and decisive nose hinted at Hellenistic art, yet he had the oval spectacles and piercing eyes of a scholar and philosopher, with the granite jaw and solid brow of a soldier. He was at once both beautiful and impossible to categorize.

"Can I help you?" Aunt Betty asked, a little suspiciously.

"No, madam. I am here to help you."

"The master is busy with another art dealer today. If you will call again tomorrow…"

"I am not here for art. I am here because of the children."

"Oh? Did Dr. Anderson send you?"

"No. I am here of my own accord."

"Are you a doctor?"

"No. You might call me a clerk."

"And just what do you know about children's dreams?"

"They're not dreams."

Aunt Betty raised an eyebrow. "I suppose you'll say they're prophetic visions or some such nonsense?"

"I'm saying you should take them seriously. Once people start remembering, they don't have long."

"I've had enough of your riddles. You are a very rude young man…" She faltered. Was he really young? He had the look of youth, but the feel of age, tremendous age. Scolding him felt like scolding her elder.

Her hand tightened on the edge of the door. "Please leave," she finally managed.

"Take my card," the man said. "I always come when I am asked for."

Aunt Betty opened her mouth to tell him that she did not want his card, but it was in her hand and he was descending the steps before she could speak. Snowflakes glittered from his dark hair as he crossed the street. No one seemed to notice him.

"Doesn't even have the decency to wear a hat," Aunt Betty grumbled as she closed the door, shivering. Returning to the parlor, she turned the card in her hand, and the firelight drew the embossed letters in flame.

I, THE ONE AND ONLY, THE SCRIBE

"Oh, Gregoire!" Aunt Betty arrested the servant as he passed by. "Why didn't you answer the door?"

"When, madam?"

"Just a minute ago. He knocked and knocked."

"That is impossible, madam."

"I also called for you."

"I assure you"—His tone adopted offended dignity—"That is completely impossible. I was in the next room. I would have heard, had there been a knock."

"Then how is it that I had to answer the door myself? Here, I even have his card."

Gregoire took the offered card and, with some perplexity, turned it back to front several times.

"I am sorry. He must have been playing some kind of crude joke. This card is blank."

"What?" The old woman snatched the card back. "It is not! See here: *I, the one and only, the Scribe*. Plain as day."

"If you say so, madam." Gregoire peered at her strangely now, and Aunt Betty felt a flutter of discomfort.

"May I get you a drink, madam?"

"Yes, please." She pressed her palm on her forehead weakly. Was the heat fever, or embarrassment? "I think I shall retire."

"Very good, madam."

Aunt Betty stared at the card, then tucking it in a pocket, began the long, weary climb up the stairs. She did not look at her portrait as she passed.

IX

The Less You Know...

"Don't look at the water," muttered Ricky as he staggered over a root. "Don't look in people's eyes. Don't look in a mirror. Don't look at a shiny coin."

"HALT!" The sudden ferocity with which Bert snapped the single word froze the two following women. Peggy and Liz retreated from the path as Bert charged past them, and planted himself directly in Ricky's path.

"You had better tell us what you know about this Scribe. Now."

Ricky's eyes flickered, and he addressed Bert's chin.

"Maybe you should too, woodsman. I noticed the news of the Scribe made no small impression on you."

"Where the Scribe walks, evil follows. I see that your knowledge goes deeper than this."

Ricky's laugh crackled like dry twigs in a fire. "If I tell you, you will die. He will find you."

"Who? The Scribe?"

"No. The Angel. The Angel follows the Scribe."

"Make sense, old man. Who is the Angel?"

"You see? You don't know. And that means that you're safe. Once you know who he is, you'll remember why he wants you. And then he'll find you."

"*You* remember. Why hasn't he found you?"

"I've remembered since I was a boy, but I was smart. I never looked in the reflections."

"He can see you in the reflections?"

"No. I can see *him* in the reflections. And if I see him, then he will come for me."

"Explain."

"I've said enough. The less you know, the less you'll remember."

Bert's silent disapproval rolled in palpable waves upon the shoulders of the old man, who avoided his gaze. At last, Bert spoke, his voice like the distant rumble of thunder.

"You said it yourself: If we must journey together, we should all be friends. Bear in mind that if you disturb the harmony of this company with your paranoia, I will abandon you in this forest and you can find your own way."

"It's not paranoia," Ricky snapped. "If you die, it's not *my* fault."

After that, a sickly silence teetered amongst the three travelers and their guide. Bert led the way, his usually light step more forceful than necessary. Liz followed, clutching her shawl around her head as though for comfort. Peggy positioned herself between Liz and Ricky, her shoulders coiled and her stride terse. Ricky lagged behind, alternating amongst gasping for breath, muttering darkly to himself, and coughing spasmodically.

The Old Forest seemed to mirror Ricky's elderly groans. Tangles of ivy and moss drifted like verdant cobwebs from the gnarled branches of the great trees. Bracket fungi dribbled in moist patterns down the trunks of trees long dead, while the path wound its way amongst the feathery sprays of ferns and crops of dark, mottled rock. Shafts of light speared through the thick foliage at intervals, transforming minute invisible insects and gossamer seed pods to dazzling confetti.

After a time, Peggy advanced to speak with Bert, and Liz found herself just ahead of Ricky.

"My dear," wheezed the old man. "May I speak with you?"

Liz hugged her shawl tighter, but nodded mutely.

"I would strongly advise you not to go to the Sender."

"Why?" Her blue eyes seemed to leap from her face, starkly contrasting with her dark hair.

"Senders are rather a mercenary bunch, if you ask me. Your Sender could take advantage of a nice little girl like you."

"I need to know where I belong."

"You belong wherever you wish to belong."

"I believe the scrivener. Somehow, I've never felt more sure of anything in my life."

"I know this scrivener. He likes to confuse people. He's an evil man."

"He did not seem so."

"I tell you, you must stay away from the Sender!" Ricky's voice rose sharply.

Bert turned, his eyes ablaze. Ricky at once withdrew, studying the shriveled leaves of past autumns at his feet.

After a few minutes, Ricky caught Liz's arm.

"I am sorry to frighten you," he said, with a ghastly attempt at a smile. "But I am very concerned that you are making a mistake."

"I think that's my business," Liz murmured, pulling back her arm.

"You're wrong." Ricky's voice hardened. "If you go to the Sender, we'll all die."

X

The Missing

"Bob, we need to talk."

Bob glanced up at Ellie and closed his electronic tablet. He rested his elbows comfortably at the tiny RV table and clasped his hands together in a posture of full attention.

"What's the subject, my dear?"

"Greta."

"The island? I reviewed her latest search history while you two talked out there."

"She told me a crazy story." Ellie related Greta's account, occasionally risking quick glances from Bob's attentive expression to the nearby bunks where RC and Greta lay inert in slumber.

"So what worries you?" Bob asked, when Ellie finished.

Ellie twisted her black hair nervously. "It's just… Whacky. Impossible."

"It's far-fetched," agreed Bob. "But many college students have stories like that. College is a time of experimentation. If, say, Greta took a little ramble with a mushroom…"

"I thought of that. So I did a little digging into Greta's background. Don't give me that look, Bob. I don't usually pry, but I was worried."

"And what did you find?"

"She went to Centaur University in Oasis, and then came straight here to study the Goric and Fulmian civilizations. Bob, she's never even been *near* Esoptron."

"Hmm. The records are pretty clear on that?"

"I thought I must have missed something, so I double-checked myself. I looked her up on Esoptron too. And that's where things got weird."

Bob leaned forward, emanating grandfatherly calm. "Weird how, my dear?"

"I found her. I actually found her—her, and her friend Christina, and her other friends."

"So her records are incorrect."

"Not incorrect. Impossible. You see, I found the information in a news article about the disappearance of Greta and her friends. The authorities were able to determine that the students had rented a boat, and two empty divers' suits washed up on the beach on one of the archipelago islands. The natives insisted that the students must have gone to the Hand of God and been eaten out of their suits by the Guardian. A few days afterward, a helicopter patrol found the boat drifting along the shoreline and, a few hours later, a body washed up on the mainland beach. It was Tina. The water had destroyed much of the evidence, but it looked as though she had endured some kind of beating. The natives said that she had been crushed by the Guardian. The five students were never seen after that."

Ellie's face shrunk like a pale onion skin, as she leaned forward and spoke in a voice tremulous with fear. "But the clincher is this. Even accounting for world time difference, that news was *over eighty years old.*"

"My dear, you're trembling. Look, there's a very rational explanation. Perhaps, as a child, Greta was interested in the story and subconsciously created an ending to it. Then it became mixed in with her real memories, ready to be triggered by something—like the picture of the island."

"Bob." Ellie didn't meet his eyes. "There's more."

"Well?"

"I found pictures of the disappeared students." Her breath caught in her throat, and she laid her tablet on the table. Upon opening, the screen revealed five faces.

Bob's face drained of color.

"I knew you had to see it," Elizabeth murmured. "First, there's the names: Christina, Richard,

Robert, Margaret, and Elizabeth. And now the pictures. Bob, those students are *us*."

XI

The Angel

A fern of snow followed Dick as he entered the house. He stomped the gray slush from his boots and knocked a light dusting from the brim of his top hat. Two servants magically appeared, one taking his coat and another his hat. Dick pinched his gloves at the tips and slid his hands free, brushing his burgundy waistcoat smooth in almost the same gesture.

"Papa!" Maggie and Ribs leaped down the stairs and flung themselves into his arms.

"Hello, hello!" Dick squeezed them both and planted a quick kiss on the top of Maggie's head. "Come see what your papa has bought. I'll give you each a guess."

"Chocolate!" Ribs' eyes sparkled.

"Something artistic, Ribs, my man. I'll let you try again."

"Oh." Ribs scuffed at a drop of slush on the floor, then squinted up at his father. "A painting?"

"Wrong! Maggie?"

"A statue?"

"Ah! My little genius!" Dick pinched her cheek. "Come see! Come see!"

"Wait for Aunt Betty!" Maggie implored, catching her father's coat by the tails before he swept away.

"Oh happy day!" exclaimed Aunt Betty, approaching from the parlor. "Another statue! I can barely contain my excitement."

Dick quickly masked the scald in his gaze, and led his children at a pace too quick for the aged woman, speaking quickly all the while.

"I had the movers place it in the gallery. It's a little too…precious…to be in the common area of the house."

He paused on the threshold of the room, his eyes darting teasingly from one child to the next. Then he threw the doors open.

A flood of light poured over the family from the wall of great windows that stretched the length of the gallery. Lifting their eyes, they beheld a pedestal draped in black velvet, upon which stood the breathlessly imposing figure of a golden angel, girt with an undrawn sword. His outstretched wings, fully sixteen feet from tip to tip, seemed to gather the light into a sphere and toss it up to the ceiling, where it shattered in a thousand glittering fragments of gold. His hands rested with delicate strength upon the pommel of his sword, as though waiting for a command to unsheath it.

"Isn't it marvelous?" Dick spoke in a cathedral whisper. "Its origin is a mystery. Someone rediscovered it in the basement of an estate of an old man long since dead. I'm working on tracing its history from there. I know it's a bit unusual, buying something whose history, age, and origin is entirely mysterious. But it was a ridiculously low price and such an unusual piece, I couldn't pass it up. Notice the condition! Gold dents easily because of its softness, but this angel—not a scratch!"

Dick turned expansively to his children. "Well? What do you think of it?"

Neither Maggie nor Ribs had moved since their first glimpse of the angel. Their gaze had frozen upon it, as though it grasped them through its blank eyes. At her father's question, Maggie sucked in a sharp breath, like a backward hiss.

"I don't like it!" she gasped, then turned and fled. The clatter of her feet ascended the stairs in the lobby, and her sobs echoed through the great house.

"What's gotten into her?" Dick blinked. "Ribs, my man, are you cold?"

The corners of the boy's mouth quivered. "I wish he would stop saying such horrible things."

"What have I said that is so horrible?" Dick knelt by his son.

51

"Not you. Him." The child's pointing finger wavered. "He was in the bathroom mirror today too."

"The statue?" Dick rose. "Ribs, that's ridiculous."

Aunt Betty pushed forward, her breath short.

"Ribs, what is he saying? What is the statue saying?"

The little boy hid his face behind his arms. "He says he's come to kill us."

XII

The Curse and the Cure

Ricky coughed breathlessly as he joined the three others at the bottom of a steep decline. "How kind of you to let me catch my breath."

Bert ignored him.

"Widowmaker," he muttered darkly.

"Widow what?" Liz asked, her eyes darting like scattered fish from Bert to Peggy.

"See that large branch?" Bert pointed. "Since it broke off—probably during a recent storm—its entire weight is now supported by that tangle of branches. If we tweak any of those lower branches in passing, which we could hardly help, the branch might fall."

"And squash us like bugs," said Ricky helpfully.

"Hence 'widowmaker'," Peggy finished. Liz hugged herself.

Bert eyed the branch. "We'll have to go around."

Peggy's eyebrows arched into question marks. "You mean, through the stinging nettles and briars?"

Bert slid a sword from the scabbard strapped to his back. "Tuck in all loose clothing and guard your face. I don't want someone getting thorns whipped into their eyes."

Dark briars tangled with the live green spikes of nettles, bristling with points that gleamed red in the filter of the setting sun. The dry briars cracked under the swoop of the blade, severed branches tangling amongst themselves. Bert, his hands gloved, pulled the branches free and threw them high over the bank of thorns. Progress was painfully slow, as the others gave Bert and his blade a wide circumference.

Peggy tugged her hair free from a briar and Liz seemed afraid to move. Ricky brought up the rear, using an oaken branch both to support himself and to thrust back the thorns.

At last, they completed the loop back to the path.

"All well?" Bert asked.

Peggy picked a thorn from the thin sole of her shoe. "All well."

"Nothing to report," Ricky called.

Liz swallowed tears. Her old stockings had been shredded, and puffy red welts criss-crossed her skin.

"It hurts," she whispered. "A lot."

"That's what stinging nettles do," Bert said dryly. "Come here, I've got a cure. Do you see this plant with the small orange flowers?"

Liz nodded.

"It's called jewelweed. It always grows next to stinging nettles, and when you crush the stalk—like so—and squeeze the juice on the sting, your pain is relieved."

Liz sighed in relief as the milky substance soothed her flesh. Bert's eyes curved into blue crescents, and a flash of white amongst the pale beard proved his grin. "You see? The evil and the good, growing together."

"That's similar to what the Sender said before he sent us," Liz said. " 'The Scribe and the Angel are like jewelweed and nettles. The curse and the cure are often very near to each other.' Remember?"

"You've seen a Sender before?" Peggy asked.

Confusion spread over Liz's pale features. "No. Why should you ask that?"

"You said that the Sender described the Scribe and the Angel like jewelweed and nettles."

Liz shriveled. "I don't know what you mean. What Angel?"

Peggy and Bert shared a quick glance. A violent tremor seized Ricky's body.

"Ricky?" Peggy gripped his shoulder.

"She's beginning to remember," the old man rasped. "If she remembers, he'll come straight here. We'll never make it out of this Forest alive."

XIII

The Empty Tomb

"Big doings next week!" Bob announced cheerfully at breakfast. "Our top investor is planning to visit, and he will have the honor of being present when we open the door of the tomb."

"About time!" Greta said around a mouthful of bagel.

"I agree!" Ellie called from outside, where she rested in a lawn chair.

Ellie breathed in the mingled aroma of her hazelnut roast as the world awoke around her. The dawn painted the dark mountains sharply against a field of orange and rose, and the fingers of a light breeze made the sparse trees musical. The flicker of an outstretched wing caught the edge of her vision, but was gone the next moment in a tangle of mountain shrubbery.

"Good morning, honey!" she called to her son, as RC trudged up the trail from the dig site. He glanced up at her, his eyes glazed with the shadow of troubled thoughts.

"Mom, when did we plan to open the tomb?"

"Next week."

"Something's wrong then. The door is open."

Bob appeared at the RV door. "What do you mean, it's open?"

"The tomb is open. Come see for yourself. Someone must have opened it in the night."

Bob swore and paused to snatch a flashlight from the windowsill. Greta followed, pulling an olive-green vest over her torso. Ellie left her coffee mug on the RV stairs as she and the others clattered down the steep, narrow trail. The steps of the ancient tomb descended into a void of darkness.

With a sharp click, Bob's flashlight illuminated the narrow chamber between the stairs and the door. The beam of light was instantly swallowed by the vast darkness beyond the open doorway of the tomb. A chill draft breathed from the open tomb.

The others clustered behind Bob as he stepped into the entry-way.

"What the…?"

No runes interrupted the perfect smoothness of the circular chamber's walls. In the center of the floor stood an octagonal pedestal of polished black stone, so deep it seemed to absorb all light. Its surface revealed the impressions of two large feet.

Behind the pedestal, a little to the left, stood a shining mirror, taller than a man, framed in scrolls of gold. Opposite the mirror, to the right of the pedestal, rose a lectern of gold, upon which a scroll had been stretched and weighted at the top and bottom by a golden quill and a golden inkwell.

"Look at the size of these footprints!" RC exclaimed. "The warrior had to be ten feet tall, at least!"

"Not necessarily," Bob pointed out. "The Fulmians may have placed the warrior's mummified body in a man-shaped casket sized larger than life, to emphasize his greatness."

Greta cast Bob a sharp glance. "Do you really believe the Fulmians did this?"

Bob did not answer.

"Why take a mummy and leave the gold?" Ellie murmured. "And if the mummy casket was golden too—as we can presume—how in the world could the thieves transport it without equipment?"

"And do it so quietly," Greta added, darkly.

Bob passed his flashlight to Greta and approached the lectern, his shadow draping over the scroll as though cut from black fabric. Reaching into his breast pocket, he retrieved his LED penlight.

"There's always a logical explanation," he muttered to himself as he rummaged in the same pocket for his reading glasses. Clearing his throat, he read aloud.

I, the one and only, the Scribe, Bringer-of-mercy, Reflection-of-life.
When death walks near, remember me.
If marked as mine, my mark shall save.
But if unmarked when found, then he
Shall mark you worthy of the grave.

"Well!" Bob said. "That's certainly cheerful."

"Look at this mirror," Ellie said. "Not a speck of dust on it, anywhere. It's like it's been newly cleaned."

"It doesn't make sense," RC said.

"It certainly doesn't."

"I wasn't talking about that." RC's voice stretched taut. "I've been looking over this door. No signs of being opened. Anyone who opened the door from the outside would have needed some kind of prying equipment. But there are no marks. And when we first entered the chamber, I noticed that, despite the lack of dust on any of the artifacts, there were footprints in the layer of thick dust on the floor. Only one set. The same size as the prints on the pedestal."

"That's absurd!" said Bob.

"Look for yourself!" RC snapped, trembling. "I'm telling you, it looks like…like…"

"Like what, RC?" Greta asked, her voice hard-edged.

The light cast RC's eyes in spectral shadow.

"Like the door was opened from the *inside*."

XIV

Mirror of Worlds

Frost licked at the edges of the windowpane. Below the window, in the garden, the frozen pond glittered as though carpeted with a thousand shards of glass. Maggie leaned against the window, her breath repeatedly appearing like the shape of a ghost on the pane, then melting into transparency.

"Maggie?" Aunt Betty called from the doorway. "Come away from the window, dear. It's time for your bedtime story. Shall we read another chapter of the *Adventures of Thomas Beaker*?"

"Yes!" Ribs shouted, bouncing on his bed. "Hurry up, Maggie!"

Maggie reluctantly slid from the window-seat and curled herself under her covers as Aunt Betty settled herself in the rocking chair between the two beds.

"Now, where were we?" Aunt Betty asked, thumbing through the yellowed pages.

"He was just preparing to go through the Valley of Snakes," Maggie reminded.

"Ah yes. The snakes. Chapter Thirteen: In which the company meets the man who saves their lives."

Aunt Betty paused, soaking up the expectation of the two children, then continued.

*   *   *   *   *

He stood, wreathed in the mists of the swamp, almost invisible save for the haunting quality of his eyes, deep in the recesses of his hood. Those eyes had seen worlds, and worlds upon worlds.

"Come inside," he said abruptly, and led the way along the boardwalk to a small log hut. Its roof was padded with moss, its logs walls crusted with lichen. A newt skittered across the front windowsill before disappearing in a chink in the wall.

"Must be cheap real estate," Richard remarked as they approached.

"Private," said the Sender. "That's all that matters."

Richard shouldered his way past Elizabeth, entering the cabin first. Once inside, with the door closed, the tension shed from their shoulders like an old skin.

"Why relax now?" said the Sender. "He can reach you as easily in here as he can out there."

All four stared at him, as he moved past his rough wooden table and chair, and stoked the fire with an iron poker.

"You know about him?" Robert asked at last, his voice dry.

The Sender threw back his hood, revealing shaggy gray hair and an untrimmed beard.

"I would be a poor Sender, if I did not. It is hard to miss the only being who is constant to all worlds and all times."

Elizabeth began to cry. Margaret seated herself in the wooden chair and stared into the fire, hugging herself. Richard paced, while Robert rubbed his jaw over and over.

"There's got to be some way to escape him!" Richard snapped.

"There are limitations to everything," Robert said. "I'm sure there is some logical way out of this."

"Like what?" Richard snarled.

"What do you suggest?" Robert asked the Sender.

Their host seated himself against the wall and crossed his ankles. "I'd like a little background information first."

Silence cocooned the room until, at last, Robert said quietly, "We visited the Hand of God—not meaning any harm, of course."

"Of course," said the Sender, a little acidly.

"We encountered"—Robert shuddered—"the Angel. He did something to our companion."

"Oh? There were five of you?"

Robert nodded. "He changed her. He made her... She was...affecting us strangely. We all went mad."

The sobriety in the Sender's expression chilled the room. "Where is she now?"

Robert glanced at his companions and replied simply, "She... She isn't with us anymore."

"I see." The weight of the Sender's gaze pressed upon them. "Then you all know why he's after you."

After a brief pause, he asked, "Have you met with the Scribe?"

"We have," Robert said cautiously.

"And...?"

"We found his terms unreasonable."

Something like anger, and a little like pity, sprang into the Sender's expression.

"Then you all will die," he said.

Elisabeth gasped with panicked sobs. Richard's jaw set.

"There's another way!" he shouted. "You know how he works. You can send me to a place where I'll be safe from him."

The Sender observed Richard, then slowly uncrossed his legs and stood. "No world is safe from the Angel."

"You can make it hard for him to find us," Margaret pointed out.

The Sender cast her a sharp glance. "Yes, I can. But it won't do any good."

"How can you do it?" Robert pressed.

"I told you, it won't do any good."

"I have money!" Richard fumbled at his pockets. "See? More than you've seen for a long time, I bet."

The Sender sighed.

"You poor fools," he muttered. "You can have all the fortunes of ten thousand worlds and it will not save you."

Richard pressed paper bills into the Sender's hand. "Just tell me how to make it hard for him to find me."

The Sender leaned against the mantelpiece. "There are two things necessary for him to find you. First: memories. He tracks you by your memories. Whatever you remember of the incident, whatever guilt you feel, whatever you recall of the Angel—he can smell it, like a hound smells blood. You must remember in order to die. It is necessary to him for you to know why you deserve the death sentence, before he kills you."

"But we were temporarily insane!" Richard spewed.

"No," said Margaret, clearly. "We knew what we were doing."

"What is the second thing he uses to track us?" Robert asked.

"Reflections." The Sender tossed a log into the fire, and it fell in a shower of sparks. "I suspect that you know a little about reflections."

"She said she was a reflection, a mirror," Elisabeth whispered.

"And so she was," the Sender said. "That's all he is too. A reflection. A reflection of who you are, at the root of yourself."

"That's ludicrous!" Richard snapped. "He's a killer. But I'm…"

He choked on his words and colored.

"You know what you are," the Sender said sharply, and seemed to bite back deadlier words. Calming himself, he spoke with leaden weight. "You must avoid the reflections. Never look at yourself—or he may look back at you. He will scan the reflections of thousands of millions of worlds and he will find your face."

"How can this be done?" Robert asked. "We will never look in the mirror again. But we can't wipe our memories."

"I can send you to another world," said the Sender. "As an infant, your memories will be deeply suppressed. You may or may not remember to avoid reflections, but he will not look back until you begin to remember."

"You mean 'unless you begin to remember,'" Margaret said.

"No. I mean until."

"We'll be separated from each other?" Elisabeth's voice expressed panic.

"Of course," Richard answered. "If we stick together, and one of us remembers, the Angel will find all of us. We have to split up."

"Fools," the Sender muttered under his breath. "Separate worlds will make no difference. He will gather you, and you will come because you cannot help it, and you will die together."

"Must you frighten the girls?" Robert said, his lips white, his hands trembling.

Margaret rose from her chair. "Please send us. We don't have any other hope."

"You don't have any hope," said the Sender. "But thank you very much for your money."

"Don't listen to him," Robert said to Elisabeth, touching her shoulder gently. She glanced up at him, tear-trails streaking reflected flame down her cheeks. Margaret shuddered.

The Sender strode to the corner of the cabin room, and the others noticed, for the first time, that a dark, shrouded shape occupied the corner. The Sender paused before it, then pulled away the black cloth. A sudden brilliance penetrated their vision from beyond the oval frame of a standing mirror. They cowered before a vision swirling with suns and planets, punctuated by the essence of lives lived and lost, and gathered as though by an invisible hand into an infinite sphere.

"World upon world," said the Sender. "Life upon life. Are you sure you wish to go forward?"

"Yes," replied Richard, courage seeping from his face. "Hurry!"

"Very well," said the Sender. "One last thing. The Scribe and the Angel are like jewelweed and nettles. The curse and the cure are often very near to each other. When you meet the Scribe, the Angel is close, but the Scribe will always communicate with you before you encounter the Angel. It would be best to accept the Scribe's offer while you can."

"Just send us!" Robert cried. Elisabeth clung to him, trembling.

"Very well," said the Sender. "I won't say 'good luck.' You won't have any. Goodbye."

Then he pulled them toward the mirror and the vortex swallowed them alive.

*   *   *   *   *

Aunt Betty dropped the book in her lap, her chest heaving. She felt a drop on the back of her wrist and, lifting her hand, realized that her cheeks were wet. Glancing up, she recognized terror on the faces of the children.

"I'm sorry," she murmured. "I don't remember that part in the *Adventures of Tom Beaker*. What's gotten into me?"

She wiped her eyes hastily. "I'm sorry, children. Perhaps we should try another book. This one has got me all ruffled. And please don't stare. It's rude."

The children remained frozen, and the hairs on the nape of Aunt Betty's neck prickled. Their eyes fixed on some point just beyond her. She held her breath and turned in the rocking chair, slowly.

There, just inside the doorway, stood the Angel.

XV

The Dream

Liz, who had been silent all through breakfast, suddenly spoke.

"I had a dream last night—about the Scribe."

All eyes instantly fastened upon her.

"What did he say?" Bert asked.

"He was the same scrivener whom I had seen before. He held a quill pen and an inkwell, and spoke quietly, but his voice made me shiver. He said the Angel was coming and that there was only one way to save me. He said each of us must be marked with the sign of the Scribe. 'You will become mine,' he said. The way he said it, I knew he meant total ownership on his part, utter reliance on mine. He asked me if I wished to be marked. I said I did not know. Then he told me to warn the rest of you—he listed each by name—and said he would always come when called for."

Ricky thrust the tip of the oaken branch into the dying coals of the fire, and a cloud of sparks hissed around the branch.

"Now you see what sort of a man this Scribe is!" he spat. "He's an opportunist. He releases an evil Angel to kill innocent people, and then offers his victims salvation at the price of all personal freedom. It's sick."

"Assuming we believe in the Angel and the Scribe," said Peggy slowly, "what are our options for survival?"

Ricky rose, his eyes hard, like diamond-points. "Avoid reflections."

Silence muffled the day's journey. Each traveler turned over unpleasant thoughts, and Ricky occasionally lashed out with his makeshift staff, striking trees or foliage with the force of enraged fear.

As they progressed, the ground became like sponge and the moss grew thicker. The path offered the only dry passage through the increasing damp of the forest. Pools of water spread at the bases of trees weighed with long strands of mossy vegetation. The water quivered with the touch of fallen leaves or the kiss of insects. The air became saturated with moisture, though cool to the skin.

"The Pools," Bert murmured. Ricky dared look only at his shoes.

An oppressiveness built around them, like the shudder of the earth upon the approach of lightning. They staggered along the path until Bert, panting, called a halt.

"Just for a moment," he said, sinking to the base of a tree that bordered the path, his head between his knees.

"May I relieve myself?" Liz asked.

Bert made a weak gesture of permission. "Don't go far."

"Me too," said Ricky. He likewise departed the path, seeking undergrowth for privacy.

Silence reigned. Peggy sipped from her flask, her eyes scanning the forest beyond the trail. Bert seemed only half-conscious.

Peggy marked the passage of a single droplet of water, which bent the leaf upon which it traveled and then pooled at the tip like a transparent pearl. It captured the image of her face, upside-down.

Or was it her face? The drop shone like lambent gold. Peggy gasped.

The Angel's vacant eyes summoned her. She saw, in every drop of the forest, thousands upon thousands, the same reflection.

Peggy flung herself away, and the drop fell to the forest floor.

XVI

Reflections of the Past

Ellie half-opened the door of the RV.

"Where is RC? I haven't seen him since we discovered the tomb. He seemed disturbed."

"I'm sorry, I haven't seen him," Bob replied. "Have you checked the stream? He likes to fish sometimes when he's chewing on a problem."

"I'll check there."

The RV door banged shut. Bob woke his tablet, which purred to life. With a flick of his finger, Bob opened his e-mail application.

A frown tweaked his face. What was this?

Bob, I'm not sure how to respond to your last e-mail. I asked for a report on your progress. I got a confession. I can only conclude that you are writing some disturbing kind of story. Please explain.

Mystified, Bob opened his folder of sent e-mails and scrolled until he found the right one. What, exactly, had he written that had so befuddled the director?

The e-mail opened.

*   *   *   *   *

The tomb is open. He has come and I know he has come for me. It is only logical. I must pay the penalty for my actions.

We waited for Tina a long time. We thought she was dead, but I did not want to give up, partially because I felt it was my duty as a gentleman to stay, and partially because I did not know how to explain her disappearance to the university and, potentially, her family.

When we first saw her, she seemed like a shimmer in the water, like a mermaid. Then she broke the surface, flinging back her hair in a spray of sparkling droplets, and swam to the boat with sure strokes. She was not naked like Margaret. Instead, she wore a gown that gleamed like a mirror, or like water.

"Where did you get that thing?" Richard snapped.

"From the One and Only," said Tina, swishing back her hair. It was hardly even wet. And that's when we saw it. The mark on her forehead. It is hard to describe. How do you describe infinity?

"What is that?" Elizabeth asked.

Tina's gaze scanned us, and I felt like she could look right through me. "When I looked into the Angel's mirror, he spoke to me."

"Who?" Margaret asked. She looked terrified.

"The Scribe."

"I thought you said you looked in the Angel's mirror. I didn't see a Scribe."

"He's the same thing," said Tina. "When I looked in the mirror, I saw myself. Have you ever seen yourself? Really seen yourself? All the little dark corners of your mind that even you don't dare to look into. All the thoughts that you stuff down every day because they scare even you."

"Well, we all make mistakes," I said uncomfortably.

"I'm not talking about the mistakes," she said. "I'm talking about our choices, our motivations, our basic nature. Even the good things we do are so saturated with ourselves. We are motivated by looking good to others, or being applauded, or feeling good about ourselves. Not by simply doing good."

"I disagree," said Elizabeth. "People are basically good."

"I thought so too," Tina frowned. "But can you say that when you take a good hard look at yourself?"

"This is stupid," said Richard. "Let's talk about the subconscious mind once we're safely away from the creepy island."

Tina looked at him like he was transparent.

"The only fear this island holds is ourselves," she said. "When I saw myself in the mirror, I knew what I was. It broke me. The Scribe said that I was a mirror; I reflected myself. Would I like to reflect something better than myself? I said I would. He said that if he marked me with his mark, I would become like him. I said I would like that. He said it would hurt and I could never go back to being what I was and I would always be his."

"What kind of sicko is this Scribe?" Richard muttered. I realized that we all talked as if the Scribe existed. Up until that day, I would have scoffed. It wasn't logical. Now, the Scribe's existence—and the Angel's—and Tina's story—seemed the most logical things in the world.

"He's not like you think," Tina said, her expression lit with delight. "He's beautiful. I would die for him."

"He's got you in some kind of spell," said Richard.

"Tell me," said Tina. "Haven't I changed?"

We all stared at her. Yes, she had changed. I couldn't keep my eyes from her. She radiated power and beauty and serenity. In comparison to the clearness of her countenance, it seemed that shadows lurked behind all of our eyes, specters that we tried to hide.

"Yes," said Elizabeth. "You have changed. You are beautiful. But I am frightened of your change too. I don't want to be marked."

"Please go see the Scribe!" Tina pleaded. "He will make you mirrors of him too."

"I am my own master!" Richard spat. "No one tells me what to do. Not even you. At one time, I wanted to go out with you, but now I don't want to!"

"You wanted to go out with Tina?" Margaret blinked.

"Sure. What's so unbelievable about that? Any woman should be glad to go out with me."

"You are so arrogant." Margaret's lip curled in disgust.

"And you are judgmental," Richard returned. "I know I'm an arrogant jerk, but it's how I get attention, and I like attention."

Richard stopped and began to tremble. "Did I just say that? I never meant to say that."

"Let's go," I said, and we cast off.

After we were underway, Richard caught my sleeve. "Robert, why did I say that just now? It was like I couldn't help saying everything I really thought. Does Margaret truly think I'm arrogant?"

"I think you're arrogant too," I replied. "I've always disliked your cursed cockiness, but I've put up with you because Elizabeth seems impressed by your bluster, and I like Elizabeth and don't want you to have her."

"Elizabeth! So that's what this is about. Well, I've always disliked your snotty attitude. 'It's all about logic.' You're exactly as arrogant as I am, you're just sneakier and more academic about it."

I opened my mouth to contradict him and said, "I know. I like to parade my knowledge because I'm not buff like you. Acting intelligent makes me feel important. Deep down, I always know that I don't have all the answers, and it bothers me. So I pretend I'm infallible, so no one will know how little I really know."

Now I began to quiver. Elizabeth was staring at me.

"You like me?" she said. "I always thought I was too stupid for you. You made me feel so inferior. So I pretended I liked Richard to make you jealous. Except that I like Richard too. I like both of you. Honestly, I would find it awfully romantic if you both fought over me."

"Elizabeth!" Margaret gasped. "That's disgusting! Turning men into barbarians!"

"Well, you feel the same way."

"Of course I do," Margaret agreed. "I would love to have scores of men fighting for the honor of being my beau. It would make me feel desirable. But I always felt it was important to pretend I didn't care about relationships, because I wanted to feel in control. Your simpering snuggly attitude toward men always sickened me, even though I envy the attention it gains you. I wish I were pretty like you."

"But I'm not pretty at all!" Elizabeth cried. "I hate myself. I hate my stringy hair. I feel fat all the time. I am always terrified that I am not pretty enough or interesting enough for anyone to love me."

"Me too!" And both women burst into tears.

Richard and I stared.

"Are women really so manipulative?" I asked.

"Are men really such swine?" Margaret retorted.

"Anyway," added Elizabeth. "We women have to get what we want and what we want is to be noticed."

"Well, I notice you all right," said Richard. "I've sometimes imagined you…"

So it went. Deeper and deeper. Every time we opened our mouths to modify or soften a previous statement, something even more hideous came out. All of our motivations came to the surface like unearthed grubs. Every word revealed more of the self that we spend every waking moment trying to disguise.

No one wanted to return to the shore now. The boat drifted in the ocean. What would happen if we returned to the shore and spoke what we really thought to every person we met? We terrified each other, but most of all, we terrified ourselves.

"Don't you see what is happening?" said Tina quietly. "You are looking into the mirror of yourselves. You are seeing what I saw."

"Why is it happening?" Margaret's voice shook. "I never looked in the mirror."

"No, but I did." Tina rose and the sun seemed to shine from inside her. "And I was marked by the Scribe. Do you know what that means? It means that I am the mirror now."

It drove me mad. She made me open myself. She made everyone see me truly. It was unbearable.

So I was the first to hit her.

*   *   *   *   *

The chair tipped and Bob found himself on the floor, pulling breath into his lungs with hoarse gasps. Every fiber of his body trembled.

"Tina," he whispered. "Tina. Oh, God, what have I done?"

A sixth sense prompted him to glance up. Through the window of the RV, sunlight caught the gleam of gold from the charcoal-colored peak of a nearby mountain. And Bob found himself staring into the infinite, blank eyes of the Angel.

Bob made across the RV in one stride, and threw open the door. He staggered back, but it was too late.

The golden sword glittered as it arced downward.

XVII

Sword or Pen

Aunt Betty shrieked and found that her scream had words.

"Scribe! Mr. Scribe! Come quick!"

Instantly, he appeared at her side, his hand taking hers. His broad frame obscured the Angel in the doorway, but the golden wings seemed to extend from his own shoulders. He wore the same white suit, and snowflakes glittered in his hair like jewels.

"You are afraid of the Angel," he said quietly.

"Yes!" said Aunt Betty. She clung to him.

"And you? Margaret? Robert?" His eyes went to the trembling forms in the beds. "You are afraid as well."

The children nodded, their blankets balled into their fists and pulled up to their chins.

"You know why he is here."

Again, all three nodded.

"Tina," said Ribs, nearly in tears.

Mr. Scribe's face seemed cast in shadow.

"There is only one way to escape the Angel. I told you about it, years ago. I gave you a choice.

You are marked for the Angel. You are his, and he has come to collect."

"The mark of Cain," Aunt Betty whispered.

"Not as you think of it," said Mr. Scribe. "Have you not read the account? Cain's mark was not to brand him as a murderer, but to mark him safe—a murderer protected. It is the mark I offer you now."

"It will make me yours," said Maggie, both hot with anger and shrill with fear. "I don't want to be yours. I don't want you to have power over me."

"It is either I or the Angel," said Mr. Scribe.

"Can't we talk to the Angel?" said Ribs. "We can make him understand that we're sorry."

"Sorry?" said Mr. Scribe. "You are still running away. Therefore you are still denying your fault."

"It was so long ago," Ribs sobbed. "I want to live!"

A tear glittered in the corner of Mr. Scribe's eye. "So did Christina, yet you judged her worthy of death. Do not judge yourself worthy of death too."

"I wasn't myself! I wasn't myself!"

"Do you remember the last time we met?" Mr. Scribe asked quietly.

Silence reigned in the room.

"I met each of you in the vortex of the worlds, as the Sender sent you through time and space. You know my words. They are burned in your memory. 'I will give you three chances, three lifetimes, to make your choice. What will you choose? The sword? Or the pen? Do not wait until it is too late.' Now your time has almost come, and I say the same. Choose quickly."

"I can't," Aunt Betty gasped. "Your price is too high."

Mr. Scribe's eyes went to Ribs and Maggie. They did not speak.

"Goodbye," he said.

Aunt Betty found that the Angel's hand had descended upon the back of the rocking chair. She shrieked and flung herself away.

The room filled with the splinter of glass, and a gust of chilly wind tore at the curtains. Below, in the courtyard pond, jagged teeth of broken ice framed the dark waters.

The children were gone.

XVIII

The Sword

Peggy gasped and collapsed to her knees.

"What's the matter?" Bert asked sharply.

"I saw something gold in one of the drops," she replied breathlessly. "And then—oh, I can't explain it. It felt like I had suddenly fallen through ice. I was clawing for the surface, and I saw a face, a golden face with blank eyes, deep in the water. It was like…" She swallowed. "It was like I died."

"There's some wizardry afoot," Bert grumbled. "And what is taking them so long?"

At that moment, Ricky emerged from the undergrowth.

"Where's Liz?" Bert barked.

"Took off," said Ricky. He twitched, and his voice seemed oddly clipped. He laughed a short, high-pitched laugh. "Scared to death. I couldn't stop her."

"I don't believe you," said Bert. "She'd be terrified to go on her own."

"Well, you're wrong," said Ricky, speaking quickly as Bert moved past him. "She's gone. You may as well let her go."

Bert ignored him. "Liz! Liz! Where are you?"

Behind him, Ricky picked nervously at his coat. "You'll never find her."

"Why?" Bert turned on him. "Why not? What have you done to her?"

A shriek reverberated through the Forest, and then the Forest swallowed it. "Bert! Bert, come quickly!"

Ricky made a mute gesture of restriction, but Bert was already gone.

Bert met Peggy at the edge of a pool of water. He choked.

A white hand drifted just below the surface of the water, like an etiolated lily. The rest of the body faded into the deep, scarlet-laced waters.

Bert fell to his knees.

"What did you do?" he gasped at Ricky, who had just arrived.

"She had remembered," he said. "She had been warned by the Scribe. Her memories would bring him here." He laughed that strange, tight laugh again. "Don't look into the pool. He may look back at you."

Peggy stepped back from the edge, white-faced, and Bert rose to his feet. His sword whispered as he drew it from his back scabbard. An icy flame kindled in his blue eyes.

"No!" shouted Ricky. "I've avoided all the reflections. I've lived this long."

"And now you die," said Bert flatly, advancing.

Ricky hissed like a cornered animal, then turned with agility surprising for the old man. Peggy watched, her throat constricted, as Bert leaped after Ricky like a greyhound after an elderly buck. Their footsteps exploded through the shallows of a murky pool, splattering dark droplets. Ricky stumbled over a root, twisting as he fell.

The sword flashed once, twice, thrice.

XIX

The Choice

Ellie met Greta on the trail.

"Have you seen RC?" Ellie fretted.

"He is in the tomb," Greta replied, strangely preoccupied.

"Oh! I will go there now."

Greta caught her arm. "He is dead."

"Dead?" Ellie stepped back. "What do you mean? How?"

"Don't you see, Ellie? It's not the warrior's tomb. It's ours."

"Stop it!" Ellie screeched. "You're frightening me."

"You always did get hysterical!" Greta snapped. "You always wanted to play the pretty coward and pretend that it wasn't you. But you were part of it! You were! You were!"

"I never did anything!" Ellie hid her face.

"That's the problem," Greta choked, half-seething, half-crying. "You didn't *do* anything. You just watched it happen while the rest of us got our hands dirty. But you wanted it to happen. You were as guilty as the rest of us. Don't think you can escape."

"I'm not strong like the rest of you," Ellie sobbed.

"Oh? And weakness is a virtue?" Greta spat. "Your inactivity was a choice in itself. That's why he's after you too."

"Stop it! Stop it!" Ellie caught the glint of sunlight on metal. "What is that? Greta, what are you doing with a gun?"

"Run, Ellie." Bitterness bled from Greta's words. "Run for your life. But it's too late. For all of us."

Ellie broke away from Greta, stumbling down the trail, half-tripping over loose stones and roots. A raven cawed raucously and abandoned his perch as she approached.

Dimly, she registered the sharp crack of a gunshot as it echoed from the mountain peaks. She did not stop.

A flicker of gold caught the corner of her vision. She did not wait. To look into those blank eyes was to see herself. Her memories. Her guilt. Her death.

Her haste propelled her forward and she saw, too late, that she could not make the turn in the trail. The edge dropped away and she fell into the vast void of the sky.

XX

Master of Fate

How she made it past the Angel, Aunt Betty did not know. One moment, she witnessed Ribs' head disappear beneath the waters of the courtyard pond. The next, she was scrambling upon her hands and knees in the upstairs hall, screaming.

That is where Dick found her.

He shook her by the shoulders. "He's here, isn't he?"

"He's in the children's room," Aunt Betty sobbed, clinging to him. He uncurled her fingers from his velveteen coat and thrust her away, disgust twisting his upper lip.

"Leech!" he snapped. "What about Robert?"

"He jumped."

Dick laughed. "The only logical thing to do, I suppose. Margaret?"

"She jumped too."

He nodded. "It ate her from the inside out. I could see it. But she was always in control. The A-plus student, the high-achiever. Admit she was guilty? Never. Me, I've never had any illusions. Yes, I killed Tina. I'm guilty. So what?"

"It doesn't bother you?"

"Everyone's just as guilty as I am!" Dick snarled. "Kill us for being human? What kind of warped justice is that?"

"If that's humanity," Aunt Betty replied. "Shouldn't we be more than human?"

"Now you sound like the Scribe. I am who I am. Maybe I'm not proud of it all, but I'll not let some scribbler tell me who to be and what to do."

"Shh!" said Aunt Betty. "He'll hear you."

"We're dead anyway," said Dick. "But I won't cower. I'll go down laughing."

"You think that's bravery?" Aunt Betty rose, trembling, to her feet. "That's madness. You're giving up your only chance."

"So are you," sneered Dick. "Why? Because you're too scared to commit. Does that make you better than me? Or worse?" He leaned against the wall and stared at the ceiling. "Go, run away, little Elizabeth. The Angel is coming to get you."

As he spoke, a streak of reflected gold threw itself against the wall, dazzling. Aunt Betty did not wait. She groped for the staircase railing, forcing her aged legs to descend the staircase. She missed a step, reached into the air, then plunged forward with a breathless cry.

When she reached the bottom of the stairs, she did not move.

Dick's laughter rang throughout the house.

"I see you. I know why you have come. What of it? I am master of my own fate! I defy you! I defy you! I defy...!"

XXI

The Last Choice

Peggy scrambled back as Bert approached. "Stay away! Stay away!"

Bert's eyes seemed too pale for the darkness of his blood-mottled face. "She shouldn't have been killed. She did nothing wrong."

"I know," Peggy trembled. "But she brought the Angel to us."

"No. *We* brought the Angel to us. He never came to harm us until we killed her."

Peggy gritted her teeth and turned away. "What were we supposed to do? She was driving us mad."

"No. We drove ourselves mad. We couldn't look at our own reflection. But now we can't escape it. It's like a mirror reflected in a mirror, and we can't get out."

Bert stabbed his sword into the sponged ground. "Margaret, we had three lifetimes to choose and we've thrown them all away. We've learned nothing."

"There's still the Scribe."

"All right," said Bert. "Then you be the first to call him. You be the first to ask him to mark you."

Peggy stared at him, still half-crouched.

Bert chuckled mirthlessly. "You see? We won't. We had all this time and we won't."

Tendons tensed in Peggy's neck. "The Scribe said we would always get another chance before we died. He lied. Liz didn't have time."

"Yes, she did. Or did you forget her dream? She could have chosen then. She delayed. She delayed until it was too late."

Bert sank to his knees, as though exhausted. "We will *all* wait until it's too late."

Peggy's fingers found the earth, clawed it, crushed it in her fists. "Why?"

"Because we would have to admit what we are. Because we would be in another's control. Because we would be changed forever."

Peggy clenched her jaw. "Will you take the Scribe's offer? You know he is good. You sensed it, as I did, every time he was near."

Bert turned his face away. "And I know I am evil. But it is more logical to die as myself than to become good because of him."

"What if that's the only way?"

"Liberty or death."

Peggy rose to her feet, her face scarlet. "That's not liberty! You think you're free because you don't bear the Scribe's mark? Look at your face in the mirror sometime, Robert! Call it human nature, but at the bottom, it's our slavemaster. If we did and

102

said half of what crossed our minds, we would reveal the monster inside us. You call that free?"

She did not look back, but she heard Bert's parting volley. "And what will you *do* about it?"

Night had begun to fall upon the forest, like a purple curtain descending. As Greta strode away, she came to a pool and recognized Liz's hand. The loose fingers seemed to point at her. Nausea crawled up her throat, and she turned back. She passed Ricky, glad that his face was turned to the earth. After a few minutes, she returned to Bert, who sat upright against the base of a tree. She registered the stain of berries on his fingers and the stare of his vacant eyes.

Her fear sharpened from lightning blue to a colorless sensation. She closed her eyes.

"I know you are there," she said. "Just tell me: Am I the last one?"

You are the last.

He was close. So close. He could breathe upon her. She could open her eyes and see him.

She kept her eyes shut.

Bert's words came to her.

"We will all wait until it's too late."

She sensed, rather than saw, the lift of the sword.

Peggy's breath whirled in her chest. Suddenly, the colorless sensation shattered.

"Scribe! Scribe!" She fell to her knees, hands over her eyes. "I know who the Angel is. He is myself, my own condemnation, my own damnation. And he is you, the justice I deserve. I am yours, only let me live!"

Her only answer was pain. It filled her body, shredded her mind, and tore her inside out. Something inside her screamed. Someone entered her soul, like a great heel that crushed the head of the screamer, and she felt the oppressive weight of death.

Then the pain receded, shrinking into a point in the front of her skull, and she realized that she felt the gentle touch of lips upon her forehead.

She opened her eyes.

His face dazzled her eyes with gold and light. Was it the Angel? Or the Scribe? She could not tell. Radiance danced from him like reflections of lightning. He was death and life, danger and safety, horror and beauty. Her master. Her rescuer.

For an instant, she caught a glimpse of her reflection in his eyes.

What was that, illuminated on her forehead like a kiss of gold?

With terror—and joy too—she recognized it. The mark of the Scribe. It was indescribable.

How could one describe eternity?

Eyes are upon me. I feel them, invisibly passing over my profile, watching the dexterity of my fingers upon the keyboard. I know his name, a name I heard for the first time this morning.

Cerberus.

I cannot see him clearly. He is just a shadow at the edge of my vision, and if I flick my gaze toward him—flash! He is gone. But he is there again, standing just outside my range of vision, watching. The form is like a man, but the features are indistinguishable.

Who is he, really?

I will ask.

Paul Graff, Literary Immersion Expert, makes up adventures for other people. He doesn't live through them himself. That is, not until the day he receives a strange request from a mysterious new client and meets an irrepressible little boy who makes impossible claims about Paul's future life. Then he finds himself in a race against an invasion that threatens to undo the entire fabric of Reality.

First Chapter from IMMERSION
By Yaasha Moriah

Paul Graff was enjoying a short story in a fiction magazine, over a cup of black morning coffee, when he felt the unsettling insect-like whisper of eyes passing over his body. In the corner of his eye, the form of the silent watcher seemed like that of a dark man—either dressed in black, or of African descent, like himself—the face indistinct, a shadow where no shadow was cast.

Paul turned sharply, and saw only the empty corner near the stove.

He shrugged and continued to read.

Presently, he flapped the magazine shut, placed his empty mug in the sink, and gargled a capful of mouthwash over the bathroom sink. Then he stepped into the slant, shadow-cubed sunlight of morning over the suburbs. Distant skyscrapers rose against the skyline like the spires of a crown, glittering like silver. He could drive there, if he wished, but he preferred the public bus. The other Literary Immersion Experts often asked him where he got his inspiration. He never told them. It was the bus—breathing in the cross-section of humanity. You had to know people to make reality for them.

Paul nodded at the elderly woman on the bus stop bench, who harrumphed back, not unkindly. The man in the gray suit did not look up from his smartphone. The community college student pored over her oversized textbook. The young couple tangled their fingers together and forgot that the rest of the world existed.

The bus squeaked gently as it pulled to a stop, and hissed as it knelt to receive its passengers. Paul found his seat—fourth down, left, by the window. He opened his mind to humanity. Somewhere, a horn beeped in a short, friendly burst, the greeting of friend to friend during the morning commute. A young boy's voice called insistently for his father. A dog barked from an upper apartment window at pigeons on the neighboring rooftop.

The bus pulled away from the curb and the city approached, the sky crowding with swooping structures of steel and glass. The Fiction Building was easy to spot, shaped like a quill resting in an inkwell—a large cylindrical base, with a curving tower that defied gravity. The neighboring public library took the shape of a giant book, open and standing on its edge, as though beckoning the world to enter its pages.

Paul stepped down from the bus onto the walkway, and passed between twin fountains to the steps of the library. The elderly librarian at the front desk greeted him.

"Good to see you, Mr. Graff!"

Paul returned her greeting with a gracious inclination of his head. The library was quieter at this time of day, which is why he always came before his office opened. Still, a few people occupied the Immersion Booths that lined the wall. The cylindrical, dome-topped structures were occupied by a single seat facing a tilted book stand, leaving the reader's back to the open doorway—a safety precaution. Sometimes immersions became too powerful, and a reader had to be rescued by one of the ever-watchful librarians.

Glancing at the readers now, Paul observed that one woman's body was almost completely transparent, the edges pulsing softly with light, as she pored over the bookstand. A perfect immersion. Paul wondered what book she was reading.

The man in the neighboring booth was not so lucky.

"Sir?" Paul took the liberty of peering into the booth. "I notice you are having some trouble."

The slightly-faded edges of the man's body sharpened and he pulled out of the immersion. He sighed.

"This is the third week I've tried immersion. I've got depression. My therapist recommended a LIE. But I can't get into it and no one seems to know the trouble, even the librarians."

"Perhaps I can help," Paul offered. "I have a little experience with Literary Immersion Experiences."

The man shrugged. "Can't hurt, can it?"

"An immersion experience requires two things," Paul explained. "One: Your personality has to be compatible with the book. If that subject just doesn't 'itch' you, you won't immerse."

"Makes sense. And the other thing?"

"The quality. The writer must have what I call 'the immersion touch.'"

"Something special, huh?"

Paul nodded. "So tell me…"

"Chuck."

"Tell me, Chuck, what sort of books did you used to enjoy as a child?"

"As a child?" the man blinked. "I wasn't much into reading. But I liked the superhero graphic novels available at the corner store."

"What attracted you to those novels?"

Chuck's response meandered, gradually sharpening as it built from hesitation to rich enthusiasm. Paul listened, nodding, smiling encouragement, then, drawing a small notebook and diminutive pen from his breast pocket, he scribbled three titles.

"I recommend starting with these," he said, tearing the sheet from the notebook. "They'll fit your personality well, and I can vouch for the authors' immersive abilities."

Chuck reviewed the list. "I'll give them a shot. Thanks for your help, man."

"No problem."

As Paul made his way toward the glass elevator, a middle-aged librarian leaned on a book cart and grinned. "He has no clue who you are, does he?"

"I'm not advertising," Paul replied.

"But I'll bet you recommended your own books in that list, didn't you?"

Paul laughed. "Only one. I don't write much for the general public."

"That's right," the librarian nodded. "You're more into the customization business, I recall."

Paul lifted a hand in a friendly farewell as he swept by. "If you ever want a custom LIE, you know where to find me."

Her laughter followed him. "I sure do!"

Just before Paul reached the elevator, a loud bass arrested him. "Paul! Yo, Paul!"

Paul paused, collected himself, and turned with a grin he hoped was polite but just short of inviting.

"Ted! Glad to see you."

Ted's corpulent figure leaked from his fitted suit just as unpleasantly as his personality leaked from his commanding posture and brazen voice.

"Paul, I had hoped to see you at the hearing." Ted's tone spoke of deep disappointment. "It was really too bad that you missed it."

"Ted, you know my feelings about LIE advertising. I would never support the bill."

"If you had at least attended the hearing, you might have learned something worth reconsideration."

"I've done my research, Ted. I'm convinced this is an unwise move."

"You're just saying that because you think it will cut into your business. But the Shakespeare study says that immersive experience professionals like us will not be affected. Fiction and advertising are two different worlds."

"Respectfully, Ted, I disagree. Writing is all one piece. If you put immersive qualities in advertising, the public will become increasingly desensitized to immersive material, forcing fiction writers to create deeper and deeper experiences. The deeper the experience, the more potential harm to the reader. You can hardly have missed the *Times* cover story last week. A man got lost in a book. It may not be possible to find a matched personality that can go as deep as he did, and pull him back. He may be lost forever. That kind of thing is very bad for business."

Ted's grin patronized. "But those cases will happen regardless of the legality of LIE advertising."

"But they'll become more frequent as immersive tolerance increases."

"Paul, Paul, think of the benefits! What if your advertisements in Fiction Forum could be immersive? You would never lack for business."

"My business is doing well enough without immersive advertising. Besides, if everything goes immersive, my ads will be competing amongst the ads for fast food, soap, cars, pharmaceuticals, and beer. How is that improving my image?"

"If the customization business goes bust, my dear Paul, your options are limited. You either have to become an immersive match consultant or publish for the general public. In contrast, if the bill passes, you can be picked up by any number of companies as a copywriter or advertising specialist. There's no end to the possibilities. Think of it, Paul! With your record, you'd have a guaranteed career."

"With my record, I already have a guaranteed career."

"You're a freelancer, Paul. Uncertainties abound in your job. You rely on your clients' appetite and cash availability. If the economy takes another downturn like last year, your clients will all switch to this." His gesture incorporated the towering bookshelves, the Immersion Booths, and the diligent librarians. "Not a guaranteed experience, but much cheaper."

"And *cheap* is what you'll get if the bill goes through," Paul snapped, no longer interested in politeness. "If immersion generalizes, I guarantee that immersion will mushroom for a few years, then implode. It will kill fiction, libraries, *and* your precious advertising. For good!"

Paul stabbed the elevator button, and stepped into the glass cylinder without so much as a farewell nod. As the elevator descended, he leaned against the interior railing and rubbed a hand over his face. There was no reason to sweat so much. He shrugged off his ivory suit coat and folded it over his arm.

Want to read the rest of IMMERSION?
Visit <u>www.YaashaMoriah.com</u> to get your copy.

If you enjoyed **REFLECTIONS**, visit
www.YaashaMoriah.com
for more fiction stories and news of upcoming titles.

Also by Yaasha Moriah:

IMMERSION
PROJECT MINERVA
PROMETHEUS